DATE DUE

GAYLORD			PRINTED IN U.S.A.

San Antonio

San Antonio

A Downtown America Book

Sally Lee

Dillon Press
New York

Maxwell Macmillan Canada
Toronto

Maxwell Macmillan International
New York Oxford Singapore Sydney

Dillon Press
Macmillan Publishing Company
866 Third Avenue
New York, NY 10022

Maxwell Macmillan Canada, Inc.
1200 Eglinton Avenue East
Suite 200
Don Mills, Ontario M3C 3N1

Macmillan Publishing Company is part of the Maxwell Communication Group of Companies.

First edition

Printed in the United States of America

10 9 8 7 6 5 4 3 2 1

Library of Congress Cataloging–in–Publication Data

Lee, Sally.
    San Antonio / By Sally Lee.
        p.   cm. — (A Downtown America book)
    Includes index.
    Summary: Describes the history, festivals, and neighborhoods of San Antonio, Texas.
        ISBN 0–89686–510–X
    1. San Antonio (Tex.)—Description—Guide-books. 2. San Antonio (Tex.)—History. 3. Historic Sites—Texas—San Antonio— Guide-books I. Title. II. Series.
F394.S2L44 1992
917.64'3510463—dc20   91–34303

To Mike and Tracy,
who made my years in San Antonio
so special

Acknowledgments

With thanks to Suzanne Satagaj and Ernie Loeffler of the San Antonio Convention and Visitors Bureau for their generous assistance.

Photographic Acknowledgments

Front Cover: James Blank
Back Cover: San Antonio Convention and Visitors Bureau, James Blank, Schlitterbahn Waterpark

James Blank (2, 12, 18, 25); Sally Lee (10, 23, 32, 46, 49, 50); San Antonio Convention and Visitors Bureau (14, 16, 42, 44); San Antonio Conservation Society, Rose Collection (21); City of San Antonio Public Information Office (28); *Texas Highways* magazine/Bob Parvin (30); Duane Zepeda (34); *Texas Highways* magazine/Jack Lewis (36); Fiesta San Antonio Commission (38, 40); The Hertzberg Circus Collection & Museum (54)

Contents

City Flag

City seal

Fast Facts about San Antonio

San Antonio: The Alamo City; the River City; the Fiesta City

Location: South-central Texas, about 150 miles (240 kilometers) northeast of the Mexican border

Area: City, 342 square miles (886 square kilometers); metropolitan area, 2,549 square miles (6,550 square kilometers)

Population: (1991 estimate): City, 999,700; metropolitan area (Bexar County), 1,384,700

Major Population Groups: Mexicans, English, French, Germans, Irish, Italians, Polish, African Americans

Altitude: 701 feet (214 meters) above sea level

Climate: Average temperature is 50°F (10°C) in January, 84°F (29°C) in July; average annual precipitation is 29 inches (74 centimeters)

Founding Date: 1718, incorporated as a city in 1837

City Flag: A white star on a red and blue background; the three colors represent the United States and Texas, which use these colors in their flags; the star is a symbol of Texas, the Lone Star State; in the center of the star is the Alamo, representing the famous battle fought in the city

City Seal: A star sits in the center of the seal, in the middle of which are scales, representing justice; the star is a symbol of Texas, and "Texas" is spelled out around the star; "City of San Antonio" surrounds the outside border of the seal

Form of Government: The city has a council-manager form of government; a mayor and ten council members are elected to two-year terms, and they appoint a city manager

Important Industries: Military, medical and scientific research, tourism, retail and wholesale trade, manufacturing

Festivals and Parades

January: Mud Festival; Los Pastores; Martin Luther King March

February: Livestock Show and Rodeo; Carnival del Rio

March: St. Patrick's Day Parade and River Dyeing

April: Fiesta San Antonio activities; Starving Artists Show

May: *Cinco de Mayo*; Armed Forces Week

June: Juneteenth celebration; San Antonio Festival

July: July 4th Fiesta

August: Texas Folklife Festival

September: *Diez y Seis de Septiembre* celebration; Labor Day Festival; Jazz SA Alive

October: Greek Funstival; Octoberfest; River Art Show

November: River Lighting Ceremony and River Parade

December: *Fiesta de las Luminarias; Las Posados*

For further information about festivals and parades, see agencies listed on page 58.

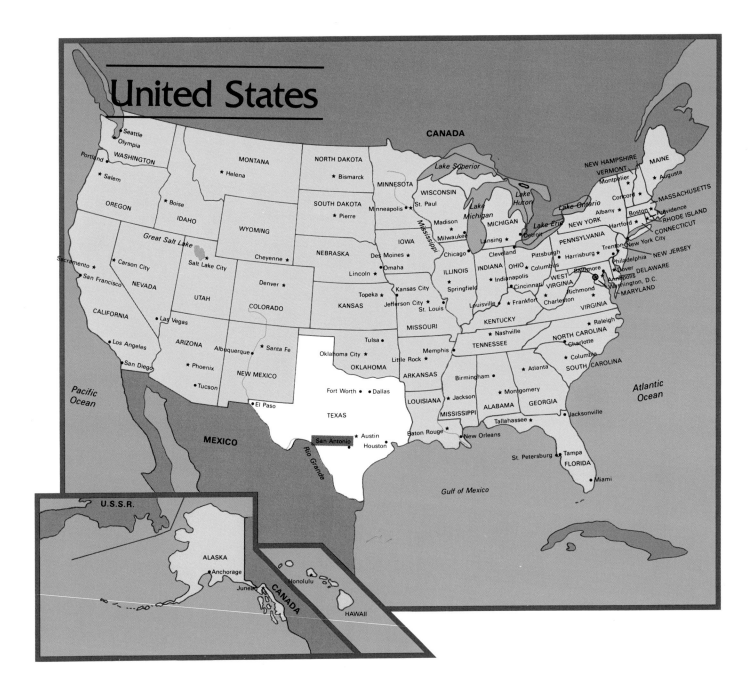

United States

San Antonio

TEXAS
San Antonio

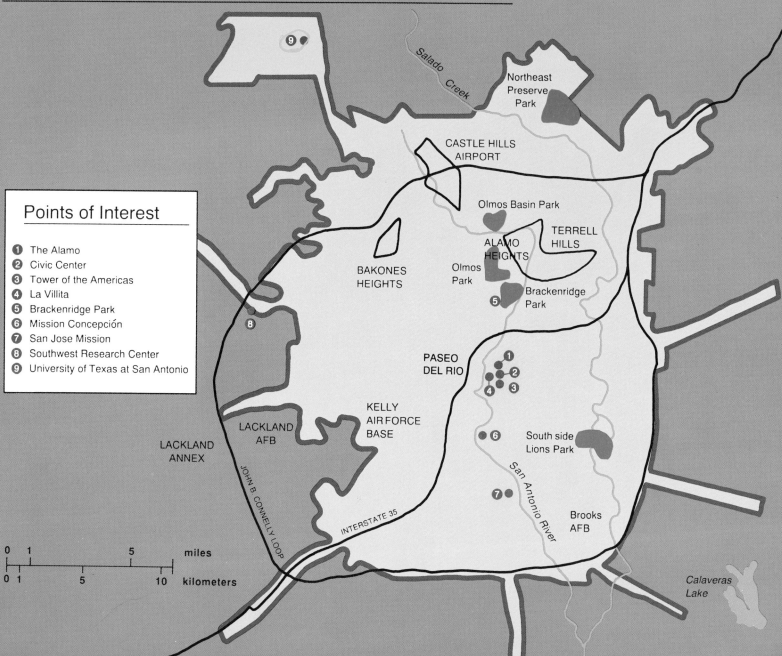

Points of Interest

1. The Alamo
2. Civic Center
3. Tower of the Americas
4. La Villita
5. Brackenridge Park
6. Mission Concepción
7. San Jose Mission
8. Southwest Research Center
9. University of Texas at San Antonio

Salado Creek

Northeast Preserve Park

CASTLE HILLS AIRPORT

Olmos Basin Park

TERRELL HILLS

ALAMO HEIGHTS

BAKONES HEIGHTS

Olmos Park

Brackenridge Park

PASEO DEL RIO

KELLY AIR FORCE BASE

LACKLAND AFB

LACKLAND ANNEX

South side Lions Park

San Antonio River

Brooks AFB

JOHN B CONNELLY LOOP

INTERSTATE 35

Calaveras Lake

| 0 | 1 | 5 | | miles |
| 0 | 1 | 5 | 10 | kilometers |

1

The Magic of San Antonio

There is magic in downtown San Antonio. The busy city can disappear in the time it takes to climb down a flight of steps. In its place is a beautiful riverside resort. The cars and buses crowding the streets above are forgotten. The blazing summer sun is lost behind the cool shade of tall cottonwood and cypress trees. This magical change is made possible by the San Antonio River.

The San Antonio River winds like a green ribbon through the heart of the city. It is lined with a 2.5-mile- (4-kilometer-) long walkway known as the River Walk, or by its Spanish name, *Paseo del Río*. Sidewalk cafés, galleries, and quiet parklike areas line the River Walk, giving downtown workers and visitors a calming break from the city above.

San Antonio is in the south-

One fun way to see San Antonio is to take a boat ride down the San Antonio River.

central part of Texas, at the top of the "tail" that hangs down into Mexico. The city is about 150 miles (240 kilometers) northeast of the Mexican border. Some people have even called San Antonio Mexico's most northern city because of the strong Mexican influence found here. Its businesses, people, and culture are all linked closely with its neighbor.

San Antonio's southern location gives it a mild climate. There is plenty of sunshine—about 300 days each year. During the summer, temperatures rise above 90°F (32°C) on most days. This is a good time for swimming or floating in inner tubes down the nearby rivers. The spring and fall have more rain, but tempera-tures remain warm, usually between 75°F and 85°F (24°C and 29°C). Even cold spells in the winter do not last long. Once in a while, a rare dusting of snow may cover the ground, delighting children who have never seen the strange white powder.

San Antonio has the charm of a small town, but it is not small. Its 999,700 residents make it the ninth largest city in the United States. When the surrounding area is included, the number jumps to more than 1.3 million people.

In spite of San Antonio's size, it is different from other large American cities. The downtown area has some modern buildings but not as many towering skyscrapers as its

A spectacular view of San Antonio at night from the top of the Tower of the Americas.

The busy restaurants and shops that line the River Walk are the heart of downtown San Antonio.

Texas neighbors, Houston and Dallas. The city honors its past and is more likely to save historic buildings than to tear them down and replace them with modern ones. San Antonio does not have big factories pouring smoke into the air, either. The city makes most of its money in nonpolluting ways. These include jobs in the military, medical and scientific research, tourism, and manufacturing.

The early Spanish explorers built forts in San Antonio, and the military has been important to the city ever since. Today it has the largest group of active military bases in the United States. The city's one army base and four air force bases provide jobs for almost 90,000 military personnel and 67,000 civilians.

San Antonio is also one of the Southwest's leading science centers, especially in the field of medical research. At the Southwest Foundation for Biomedical Research, scientists work on ways to detect, cure, and prevent human diseases. They have the world's largest colony of baboons to help them with their research.

Another important source of jobs in San Antonio is tourism. With over 10 million visitors a year, San Antonio is the only large city in Texas that counts tourism as a major industry. Taking care of the city's visitors provides jobs for almost 30,000 people.

Many San Antonio residents work for the 1,300 manufacturing firms in the city. These companies make aircraft parts, oil field equipment, clothing, electronic goods, cement, food products, and medical supplies. Several of these products are exported to Mexico. The city is also the chief outlet for many of the fruits, vegetables, and nuts grown in the surrounding countryside.

Much of San Antonio's charm comes from its colorful mixture of people. More than half of the city's residents are Hispanic. Most of them are Mexican Americans. They are

responsible for many of San Antonio's traditions. The area was also popular with German settlers, and many people still carry on their ancestors' traditions. Yet in spite of its ethnic mixture, San Antonio has very few racial problems. When World War II ended in 1945, the military bases were integrated. In other words, blacks and whites were able to live in the same area. This integration spread peacefully into the schools and other places.

San Antonio has a spirit all its own. It is seen in the festive *El Mercado,* or Mexican Market, the charming 18th-century village of La Villita, the spirited ten-day celebration of Fiesta San Antonio, and in the beauty of its Christmas traditions. Will Rogers, a popular American humorist and performer in the early 1900s, named San Antonio one of the four "unique" cities in the United States. It has proven to be a fitting description of this special city.

El Mercado, or Mexican Market, celebrates the traditions of San Antonio's large Mexican-American community.

2

"Remember the Alamo!"

The situation looked hopeless. For ten days in 1836, the band of 157 men inside the Alamo had held off Santa Anna, the Mexican dictator, and his 5,000 soldiers. This small group of men, under Lieutenant Colonel William Travis, made up San Antonio's entire military force. Seeking help, Travis sent messages to nearby towns. The only ones to respond were 32 men and boys from the town of Gonzales. They slipped through enemy lines at the last minute.

According to legend, Travis called his men together. After explaining their desperate condition, he pulled out his sword and drew a line in the dirt. "Those prepared to give their lives in freedom's cause, come over to me," he said.

Every man except one crossed

Each year many people visit the Alamo, the site of the bloody battle between the forces of Colonel William Travis and Santa Anna's raiders.

the line. Among those who chose to fight were Davy Crockett and his "Tennessee Boys" in their coonskin caps. Colonel James Bowie, who was too sick to stand up, insisted that his cot be carried over the line.

The men in the Alamo held off the Mexican army for two more days. Then, before dawn on March 6, 1836, the siege ended in a brief but bloody battle. It began when Mexican bugles sounded the dreaded *degüello*, meaning that no lives would be spared. Thousands of Mexican soldiers stormed the walls from all directions and finally broke through. When the fierce struggle was over three hours later, all but six of the Alamo defenders lay dead. Santa Anna ordered these men killed also.

The 189 Texans had managed, however, in their last hours of life, to kill nearly 1,600 of Santa Anna's men.

The Battle of the Alamo was the most dramatic and famous moment in San Antonio history. Yet the area had been a busy place for more than 100 years before that event.

Native Americans were the first people to live along the banks of the San Antonio River. They were there long before the Spaniards reached their village of Yanaguana on June 13, 1691. That day happened to be the feast day of Saint Anthony of Padua. In honor of their saint, the Spaniards renamed the village and nearby river San Antonio.

The city got its official start in 1718 when the Spanish built a

The Alamo as it looked in 1849, when it was used as a quartermaster depot.

Catholic mission there. Its purpose was to convert the Native Americans to Christianity. Originally called *San Antonio de Valero*, it was later called *Alamo*, the Spanish name for the cottonwood trees surrounding the monastery and church. The Spanish also built a fort nearby to protect the mission from attacks by Apache and Comanche Indians and to keep the French from taking over the area. Later on, the Alamo was sometimes used as a fort. This now-famous structure marked the beginning of the city of San Antonio. But the first settlers did not arrive until 1731 when the Spanish king sent over people from the Canary Islands.

In 1821 Mexico won its independence from Spain and San Antonio came under Mexican rule. But the Texas settlers, many of whom had come from the eastern United States, didn't want to be ruled by Mexico. They revolted by fighting several battles in 1835 and 1836, including the Battle of the Alamo. Sparked by cries of "Remember the Alamo!," General Sam Houston and his army of some 800 angry Texans defeated the Mexican army six weeks later at the Battle of San Jacinto. This marked the beginning of the Republic of Texas.

Texas joined the United States in 1845 but dropped out of the Union in 1861 to join other southern states in the Confederacy. Although no Civil War battles were fought in San Antonio, the city was used as a supply center for the Confederate forces.

After the Civil War, around 1866, some cattlemen started rounding up the millions of cattle that had multiplied from stock left by the Spaniards. San Antonio became the first cow town of the old West. Young men signed on to drive huge herds 800 miles (1,288 kilometers) up the Chisholm Trail to the railroad in Abilene, Kansas.

During the days of the cattle drives, businesses sprang up to trade hides, wool, and supplies with cattle ranchers. One of these new products was barbed wire. It was shown in public for the first time in San Antonio.

San Antonio became more of a military town in 1876 when Fort Sam Houston was built. Ten years later, the great Indian warrior Geronimo and 30 other Apaches were held as prisoners for 40 days in the area of the base called the Quadrangle.

San Antonio was somewhat cut off from the rest of the United States until 1877, when a small, independent railroad finally reached the city. The discovery of oil in the late 1800s also helped the city to grow.

In 1910 Lieutenant Benjamin D. Fulois arrived at Fort Sam Houston and was told to teach himself to fly. His first flight lasted a little more than seven minutes, but it was enough to mark the birth of military

The clock tower of the Fort Sam Houston Quadrangle, where Geronimo and his men were held prisoner.

flight in the United States. In 1917, two airfields, Kelly Field and Brooks Field, were opened so that the army could train pilots for World War I. Soldiers also poured into the city for training before going to Europe to fight in the war. By 1920, San Antonio's population had reached 161,000, making it the largest city in Texas at the time.

By the 1920s the San Antonio River had become a dumping ground for trash. City leaders wanted to pave the river over and use it as a sewer. Fortunately, some people fought to keep this from happening. During the Great Depression in the 1930s, when many people all over the United States were out of work, the government hired unemployed peo-ple, through the Works Project Administration, to build special pro-jects. In San Antonio these workers cleaned out the river and built rock walls, bridges, and dams. They cre-ated the beautiful River Walk that San Antonio is known for today.

When the United States entered World War II in 1941, San Antonio again became an important area for training military men and women. Thousands of pilots, navigators, and gunners trained at Brooks, Kelly, Lackland, and Randolph airfields. Soldiers in the army trained at Fort Sam Houston.

After World War II, parts of San Antonio continued to prosper, but conditions became worse for the poor. By the 1960s, thousands of

Downtown San Antonio got a much needed facelift when many of its old buildings were torn down to make room for the HemisFair Plaza.

Hispanic and black families lived in tiny houses built around outdoor public toilets. They had no paved streets or sidewalks and nothing to stop floodwaters from driving them from their homes. These neighborhoods were so poor that Peace Corps volunteers trained there to learn about the conditions they would find in Latin America.

Then the city made some improvements. In 1968 San Antonio celebrated its 250th anniversary by hosting a world's fair, called HemisFair. To make room for HemisFair, some of the downtown slums were cleared away. The people who lived there were given money to find better housing. New buildings were added, including the Tower of the Americas, a large convention center, and the Arena. More hotels were built and improvements were made to the river.

Conditions began to improve also for Hispanics and blacks. Before the 1970s most of the city's decisions had been made by wealthy white businessmen. Then Hispanics organized to get more political power. They used their political strength to see that they got their fair share of city services. The poorer areas, where many of the Hispanics and blacks lived, finally got the streets, sidewalks, and flood control that they needed.

In 1981, city residents elected

Henry Cisneros as their mayor. He became the first Mexican-American mayor of a major city in the United States. He was popular enough to be reelected three times before he chose not to run for office in 1989.

During the past twenty years San Antonio has grown and changed. In spite of this growth, much of the population is still poor. Many people have come from Mexico, either legally or illegally, hoping to find a better life. They haven't always found it. Many of these immigrants live in shacks because they cannot afford anything better.

The large number of children from Spanish-speaking homes makes education a problem, too. Some chil-dren have trouble learning in English, the language used by most of their teachers. As a result, over a third of Mexican-American children drop out of school. In the inner-city schools, as many as 42 percent of the students drop out. Without an edu-cation, they have problems finding jobs, and many get into trouble with the law. Today the city and private businesses are working harder to improve education and keep chil-dren from dropping out of school. Some businesses send volunteers into the schools to tutor students who are having problems. They also serve as role models. Since the late 1960s, preschool children have been helped by the Head Start program. This pro-

Henry Cisneros was the first Mexican American to be elected mayor of a major U.S. city. He governed San Antonio for eight years.

gram works with poor children to give them extra help in getting ready to start kindergarten.

In spite of its problems, San Antonio residents think their hometown has a bright future. Most of its present industries are strong, and more scientific industries are being developed. If its future can be as rich as its past, San Antonio will continue to be a special city.

3

A Patchwork of Neighborhoods

Like a patchwork quilt, San Antonio is made up of many different neighborhoods. Each one is home to people of similar ethnic backgrounds and economic levels. Clusters of neighborhoods make up the various "sides" of the city.

The houses on the north side belong mostly to white business and professional people. They range from small, middle-class homes to large and expensive estates. Many have their own swimming pools and tennis courts. Some of the wealthier communities are built around their golf courses.

Several small neighborhoods on the north side feature fine older homes. Some of these are quite large. Many of the lawns are filled with huge, old trees that almost hide the houses behind them. Communities

San Antonio is made up of many different neighborhoods, each with a unique style that comes from the people who live there.

A home in the historic King William district

such as Olmos Park, Castle Hills, Alamo Heights, and Terrell Hills are popular with professional people and those who have retired from the military. Another wealthy neighborhood, close to downtown, is the King William historic district. In the 1800s, this was the most elegant area of the city. It was home to prosperous Germans. Most of these homes have been restored.

Most of the people in the military

live all over the city, but some families choose to live on the bases. Children who live on military bases are used to hearing fighter jets roar over their heads, or seeing military helicopters landing near their homes. Three of the bases—Fort Sam Houston, Lackland, and Randolph—have their own school districts for the children who live there. These children have a number of things in common. Most of them have moved around a lot and have attended many different schools. Many have lived in other countries.

Of all the groups contributing to San Antonio's culture and traditions, Mexicans have made the greatest impact. More than 54 percent of San Antonio's residents are Mexican American. Whether it is the conversations in Spanish heard on the street, the lively music ringing through the air, or the aroma of spicy cooking, it is hard to miss the strong Mexican influence.

A large number of Hispanics live in *barrios*, or Spanish-speaking neighborhoods, on the city's west and southwest sides. Many of the barrios are poor, but they are different from the low-income areas found in most other cities. There are no tenements, row houses, or tall apartment buildings for the poor. In San Antonio's barrios, the houses may be small and run down, but they usually have their own small yards. The west side also has neighborhoods with tree-shaded streets, picket fences,

porches full of houseplants, and brightly painted houses trimmed with fancy ironwork. You may find street vendors selling fruit, *tamales* (meat-filled cornmeal dough steamed in a corn husk), Sno-Kones, and corn on the cob from the back of their trucks.

Many Mexican games and traditions are popular all over the city. One favorite game at children's parties is the breaking of a *piñata*. A piñata is a colorful, papier-mâché figure, such as an animal, filled with candy. It is hung from the ceiling or a tree branch. Blindfolded children take turns batting at the piñata with a stick. When the piñata breaks open, everyone scrambles to pick up the spilled candy.

The Mexican influence is also seen in the foods popular in the city. Some of them are typically Mexican, while others have been changed to "Tex-Mex" cooking. One example of Tex-Mex food is chili, which is said to–have been invented in San Antonio.

A common Mexican food is the *tortilla*, a flat piece of corn or flour dough that serves the same purpose as bread would in an American meal. Tortillas are not made in bakeries; they are made in tortilla factories.

San Antonio is filled with Mexican restaurants. Many still use old family recipes for *enchiladas* (tortillas filled with meat or cheese and covered with a sauce); *fajitas* (strips of grilled steak or chicken rolled up

This house on San Antonio's west side reflects a strong Mexican influence.

A rider in the annual Juneteenth parade.

in a tortilla); and *tacos* (tortillas wrapped around a filling of spicy beef or chicken). Most meals are accompanied by *frijoles* (beans) and rice. For dessert there may be flan (Mexican custard) or *buñuelos* (thin pastries dusted with cinnamon and sugar).

Many kinds of foods other than Mexican are popular in San Antonio. The Western influence has made barbecued food popular, too. Some barbecue restaurants smoke beef brisket all day over a slow fire, then top it off with a spicy sauce. Sausage is another popular barbecue item. Add a pot of pinto beans, and you have a meal with the true taste of Texas!

Hispanics are not the only ethnic group in San Antonio. African Americans make up about 7 percent of the city's population. Neighborhoods on the east side of the city, close to downtown, are home to large numbers of black families, many of whom live in low-income housing.

The black residents of San Antonio celebrate one special holiday in addition to many others. Picnics, speeches, and parties are all part of "Juneteenth." This was the day, June 19, 1865, the slaves in Texas learned that they had been freed by President Lincoln's Emancipation Proclamation.

San Antonio's patchwork of neighborhoods gives a lively look and feel to the city. Although each ethnic group has its own customs and traditions, the different activities are enjoyed by everyone. People of all backgrounds can be found tapping their feet to German "oompah" bands, dyeing the river an Irish shade of green on St. Patrick's Day, or wearing colorful Mexican clothing. San Antonio has blended the traditions and cultures of its different ethnic groups into something the entire city can enjoy and be proud of.

4

¡Viva Fiesta!

A boy smashes an eggshell over his friend's head and laughs as confetti spills out. *"¡Viva Fiesta!"* he yells as he runs off to find his next victim. His friend isn't mad. Being hit with a *cascarone*, or confetti-filled eggshell, is part of the fun of Fiesta San Antonio.

For ten days every April, Fiesta turns San Antonio into one big party. It always occurs the week of San Jacinto Day, April 21, celebrating the day Texas won its independence from Mexico. Although Fiesta has some serious moments, such as a ceremony at the Alamo to honor the men who died there, it is mainly a time of fun and celebration.

Three big parades take place during Fiesta. The Battle of Flowers Parade is the largest and oldest. Most schools and many downtown busi-

A young San Antonio resident enjoys an ice cream during Fiesta.

One of the many floats that make up the Battle of Flowers Parade.

nesses are closed the day of the parade so that everyone can attend. The Battle of Flowers Parade has an interesting history.

In 1891, a group of women decided to have a parade for President Benjamin Harrison's visit to the city. They chose to pattern their parade after a "flower battle" one of the ladies had seen in France. It rained the day the parade was scheduled, so the president never saw it.

But a few days later, carriages decorated with flowers, floats drawn by horses, and mounted cavalry paraded around downtown. As the parade ended at Alamo Plaza, the women in the carriages threw flowers at each other. The name "Battle of the Flowers" stuck, but flowers are no longer thrown.

The River Parade, held at night, has floats that really float. People line the banks of the San Antonio River and hang over bridges to watch the decorated boats glide by.

The last parade, called Fiesta Flambeau, is also held at night. All the floats are lit up, and even the marching bands carry flashlights or flares.

Two kings rule over Fiesta—King Antonio and *El Rey Feo* (The Ugly King). Besides the kings and parades, Fiesta includes balls, queens and duchesses in fancy gowns, fireworks displays, sports events, concerts, and carnivals. During the four nights of "A Night in Old San Antonio," thousands of people squeeze into La Villita. In this recreation of an 18th-century village, they can find food, games, and entertainment from many different ethnic groups.

While Fiesta is the largest festival in San Antonio, it isn't the only one. There are so many ethnic celebrations, parades, and art and music festivals that it is hard to find a week when something isn't happening.

In February, the whole city goes

A cowboy tries to hang on during the Livestock Show and Rodeo.

Western during the Livestock Show and Rodeo. For 12 days there are rodeo performances, country and western singers, animal judgings, and auctions.

A week or so before the rodeo starts, trailriders begin their long journey to San Antonio. These groups of men, women, and children from towns surrounding the city come the old-fashioned way—by horseback and covered wagon. By day, they ride along the sides of roads. At night, they camp out on ranches or in parks. They spend their evenings eating, dancing, and recounting tales of other trail rides they have been on. On the rodeo's opening day, hundreds of trailriders parade through the streets of downtown in the Rodeo Parade.

There are two holidays during the year that celebrate events in Mexican history. The first is *Cinco de Mayo* (the fifth of May), which honors an important Mexican victory over French troops in 1862. An even bigger celebration is held on *Diez Y Seis de Septiembre* (the 16th of September), Mexican Independence

Day. It was on that date in 1821 that Mexico won its independence from Spain.

The Christmas season is one of the loveliest times of the year in San Antonio. It officially begins on the Friday after Thanksgiving, when thousands of people line the river at dusk. Suddenly, a switch is turned on and 50,000 colored lights begin twinkling in the large trees alongside the river. A lively holiday river parade follows the ceremony.

The river is even more stunning on the first three weekends in December, during the *Fiesta de las Luminarias* (Festival of Lights). On these weekends, the riverbanks are lined with thousands of candles set in sand inside small paper bags. The

luminarias, or lights, are a tradition carried over from 16th-century Spain. The tiny lanterns represent the lighting of the way for the Holy Family.

Another Christmas tradition is a procession called *Las Posadas* (the Shelters). It represents Mary and Joseph's search for an inn in Bethlehem. Some Hispanic neighborhood churches have their own posadas, but the largest one is held by the San Antonio Conservation Society, along the river.

During the posadas, two children dressed as Mary and Joseph walk along the river. Behind them follow young people dressed as angels or shepherds. Anyone who wants to join in may follow the young people.

Each year, the pageant of *Las Posadas* reenacts the story of Mary and Joseph's search for an inn in Bethlehem.

Everyone carries candles and sings as they walk along. At each stop they sing a song asking for lodging, but they are turned away by other singers. They are finally welcomed at the beautiful nativity scene at the Arneson River Theater. A party follows with food, piñatas, Christmas carols and music by *mariachis* (traditional Mexican street bands).

San Antonio is a fun-loving city that even celebrates some unpleasant things. Each January, when the river is drained so that the banks and riverbed can be cleaned and repaired, a Mud Festival is held. There are a Mud King and Queen, mud sculpture contests, and all sorts of dirty delights! It shows how far some people in San Antonio will go to find a reason to enjoy themselves.

5

Just for Fun

Whether you want to pet a dolphin, ride a trolley to a Mexican market, or make faces at a cage full of monkeys, San Antonio is for you. There is always something to do or see.

San Antonio's mild climate makes outdoor activities popular. Many of the city's 70 parks have hiking and biking trails. Golf and tennis can be played almost every week of the year. There are football, baseball, basketball, and soccer teams for kids of all ages, as well as for adults. Sports-lovers can also watch the San Antonio Missions play baseball or the Spurs play basketball.

For people who want something calmer than sports, there are always concerts, plays, and other events being held. Some residents like getting dressed up to attend the San Antonio Symphony. Others prefer

Visitors enjoy an elephant ride at the San Antonio Zoo.

the casual Brown Bag Days, a series of free summer concerts put on in the downtown parks during lunchtime. Some of the military bands also give free concerts. Other people like to sit on the grass seats of the outdoor Arneson River Theater and watch live performances on a stage on the other side of the river.

San Antonio has a very active downtown area. Driving downtown can be confusing, but there are fun ways to get around. River taxis take people to places along the water, while horse-drawn carriages make tours of the area. The most efficient way to get around, though, is to climb on a bus that looks like an old-fashioned trolley. It costs a dime and can get passengers to most parts of downtown.

San Antonio's most famous attraction is the Alamo. Actually seeing the buildings and displays at the Alamo gives a visitor a better understanding of what happened during the mission's most famous moments. An even better way to learn about the battle is to watch the movie *The Alamo . . . the Price of Freedom* at the IMAX Theater in the nearby Rivercenter Mall. The sights and sounds of the battle are brought to life on a screen six stories high.

The Alamo had been abandoned as a mission long before its famous battle. But San Antonio had four other missions that are still active

The Arneson River Theater is a popular spot for seeing concerts and plays.

Catholic churches. They are part of the San Antonio Missions National Historic Park. All four are interesting, but Mission San Jose has the most to see. By exploring the old grist mill, the Indian dwellings, the workshops, and the church, visitors can get a feeling for what mission life was like in the 1700s. A traditional mariachi mass is held at Mission San Jose for both parishioners and visitors.

Another popular downtown spot is HemisFair Park. Rising from the center of the park is the 750-foot (228-meter) Tower of the Americas. Glass elevators whisk people to the top, where they can get a bird's-eye view of the city from the revolving restaurant or the observation deck.

Another part of HemisFair Park is the Institute of Texan Cultures, a very special museum. The exhibits tell the story of the many different kinds of people who settled in Texas. An expert on American Indians might gather children around a tepee and let them handle objects the Indians once used. A cowboy may open up the chuck wagon and show what life was like on the cattle trails. Slide shows and movies are shown on the domed ceiling in the center of the museum. For four days in August, the institute hosts the Texas Folklife Festival, featuring the foods, dances, and crafts of various ethnic groups.

Downtown from HemisFair Park

One of the oldest missions in Texas, Mission San Jose still offers vistors a taste of what life was like in the 1700s.

is Market Square, which is patterned after a Mexican market. It is located on the same spot as San Antonio's first public market. In those days, farmers brought in carts of fruits and vegetables to be sold. At night, the "Chili Queens" would set up their stands to sell a mixture of spicy meat and beans called *chili con carne*, or chili with meat. Although the Chili Queens are gone now, merchants still appear nearly every weekend to sell various foods and Mexican products, and farmers still sell produce to the public from the large, covered Farmer's Market.

In Market Square there are many shops and restaurants with a definite Mexican flavor. Inside a large air-conditioned building is El Mercado, a bustling Mexican marketplace. Vendors are crowded together, each selling handicrafts, straw, pottery, clothing, and other Mexican goods.

There are many other interesting things to see in San Antonio, including its museums. The Hertzberg Circus Museum has unusual circus posters and pictures, a scale model of a circus, and the small carriage that belonged to Tom Thumb, a man who was only 25 inches (64 centimenters) tall.

Natural history comes alive at the Witte Museum. In its Eco Lab, children can watch birds hatch or study bees at work in real beehives. On Saturdays, volunteers take out some of the animals—such as the giant Texas toad, a tarantula, and a number of snakes—for the bravest visitors to touch.

Another fun place to go is Brackenridge Park. It is the home of the San Antonio Zoo, considered one of the top ten zoos in the country. Children can pet the animals at the Children's Zoo and even ride an elephant. Visitors to Brackenridge Park can also ride a miniature train named the Eagle. Or they can take a skyride and skim over the tops of trees to the beautiful Japanese Tea Gardens.

Even though San Antonio is not on the ocean, it has the largest marine park in the world. At Sea World of Texas, Shamu and other killer whales perform in a tank filled with man-made seawater. Visitors to Sea World can feed dolphins; laugh at the waddling penguins; watch performances by fish, mammals, and people; and visit giant aquariums containing thousands of sea creatures, including sharks. Sea World is more than just a place for entertainment, however. Much research takes place here to explore more about marine life.

San Antonio's latest attraction, Fiesta Texas, a musical theme park, is scheduled to open in the spring of 1992. Different areas of the park will focus on the music and history of San Antonio and south Texas. The park will honor the region's Hispanic heritage, German influence, cowboy history, and its rock 'n' roll and

country-western roots. There will also be thrill rides, restaurants, shops, and walkways.

The rolling hills and winding rivers north of the city also provide fun for San Antonio residents. Some people like to ride in canoes, rafts, or inner tubes down the rivers. Others like the more exciting set of *Schlitterbahn*, which means "slippery road" in German. This is a water park in New Braunfels, about 30 miles (48 kilometers) north of San Antonio. Here, water from the Comal River carries inner-tube riders through gentle drops and swirling whirlpools. The most daring people can ride a sled that speeds down the roof of a building and skids across the pool below.

Jingles the Elephant guards the entrance to the Hertzberg Circus Museum.

San Antonio is a mixture of many different things. It is one of the oldest cities in Texas, yet it is full of modern buildings and industries. Its military bases make it important to the United States, yet its traditions give it a strong link to Mexico. Its people value the city's past, yet they work hard to improve its future. All these things make San Antonio a pleasant city to live in, work in, and visit. It truly is a magical city.

Places to Visit in San Antonio

Museums

Hertzberg Circus Museum
210 Market Street
(512) 229-7810

McNay Art Museum
6000 North New Braunfels
(512) 824-5368
A mansion containing modern art displays

San Antonio Museum of Art
200 West Jones Avenue
(512) 829-7262

Witte Museum
3801 Broadway
(512) 829-7262
Natural history and science museum

Cowboy Museum and Gallery
209 Alamo Plaza
(512) 229-1257
Authentic cowboy objects portray the history of the cowboy

Parks

Brackenridge Park
(Main entrance is the 2800 block of North Broadway)
San Antonio Zoo
3903 North St. Mary's Street
(512) 734-7183

Japanese Tea Gardens
3800 North St. Mary's Street
(512) 821-3000

San Antonio Missions National Historic Park:
(Mission Park headquarters: 2202 Roosevelt Avenue.
Telephone: (512) 229-5701)

Mission Concepcion
807 Mission Road
(512) 229-5732

Mission San Jose
6539 San Jose Drive
(512) 229-4770

Mission San Juan Capistrano
9101 Graf
(512) 299-5734

Mission San Francisco de la Espada
10040 Espada
(512) 627-2021

Special Places

River Walk
Downtown San Antonio
Paseo del Rio Association
213 Broadway
(512) 227-4262

The Alamo
300 Alamo Plaza
(512) 225-1391

La Villita
418 Villita
(512) 299-8610

HemisFair Park:
(Park's main entrance is 206 South Alamo.
Telephone: (512) 299-8576)

Tower of the Americas
600 HemisFair Park
(512) 299-8615
Restaurant and observation deck

Institute of Texan Cultures
801 South Bowie
(512) 226-7651
Texas history and culture

Mexican Cultural Institute
600 HemisFair Park
(512) 227-0123
Mexican history and culture

Market Square
514 West Commerce
(512) 299-8600

Sea World of Texas
10500 Sea World Drive
(512) 523-3611 or (800) 422-7989

Schlitterbahn
400 North Liberty Street
New Braunfels, Texas
(512) 629-3910

Theaters

Plaza Theater of Wax/Ripley's Believe It or Not! Museum
301 Alamo Plaza
(512) 224-9299
Historical and famous wax figures

Arneson River Theater
418 Villita
(512) 299-8610

IMAX Theater
Rivercenter Mall
849 East Commerce
(512) 225-4629

Additional information can be obtained from these agencies:

San Antonio Convention and Visitors Bureau

Write to:
121 Alamo Plaza
San Antonio, TX 78205
or
P.O. Box 227
San Antonio, TX 78298
Telephone: (512) 270-8700

Greater San Antonio Chamber of Commerce

Write to:
602 East Commerce
San Antonio, TX 78205
or
P.O. Box 1628
San Antonio, TX 78296
Telephone: (512) 229-2100

Visitor Information Center
317 Alamo Plaza
San Antonio, TX 78205
(512) 270-8748

San Antonio: A Historical Time Line

1691   Spaniards first visit American Indians along the San Antonio River

1718   Spaniards found the mission, San Antonio de Valero, now known as the Alamo; Fort San Antonio de Bexar is built near the mission

1731   Canary Islanders sent by the Spanish king arrive to settle San Antonio

1821   Mexico wins its independence from Spain, placing San Antonio under Mexican rule

1836   The Alamo falls to the Mexican army; Texas wins its independence from Mexico at the Battle of San Jacinto

1837   San Antonio is incorporated as a city

1872   Barbed wire—a new product for cattle ranchers—is shown in public for the first time in San Antonio

1876   Fort Sam Houston is established by the United States Army

1891   The first Fiesta and Battle of Flowers Parade is held to honor President Benjamin Harrison

1910   Military aviation is born at Fort Sam Houston

1917   Kelly Field and Brooks Field are built to train pilots for World War I

1930   Randolph Field opens to train pilots

1939–1942   Works Project Administration construction of the River Walk

1961   Voters in San Antonio elect Henry B. Gonzales the first Hispanic to serve in the U.S. Congress

1968   A world's fair, called HemisFair, opens to celebrate San Antonio's 250th birthday

1981   Henry Cisneros is elected the first Hispanic mayor of a major American city

1983	San Antonio is designated by the National Municipal League as one of the All-American cities
1987	Pope John Paul makes a historic visit to San Antonio
1988	Sea World opens the largest marine park in the country in San Antonio
1991	San Antonio celebrates 100th anniversary of Fiesta San Antonio

A San Antonio Glossary

barrio (BAHR-ee-oh)—neighborhood

buñuelos (boon-WAY-lohs)—crisp dessert pastries sprinkled with cinnamon and sugar

cascarone (kahs-kah-ROH-nay)—a confetti-filled eggshell

Cinco de Mayo (SEEN-koh DE MEYE-oh)—"fifth of May"; a holiday to honor an important Mexican victory over French troops in 1862

degüello (day-GAY-oh)—"beheading"; Mexican bugle call to battle that signals no lives are to be spared

Diez y Seis de Septiembre (dee-AIS ee SAIS DAY sehp-tee-EHM-bray)—"sixteenth of September"; Mexican Independence Day

El Mercado (EHL mair-CAH-thoh)—"the market"; a marketplace in San Antonio

El Rey Feo (EHL RAY FAY-oh)—"the ugly king"; in San Antonio, he presides over Fiesta events

enchilada (ehn-chee-LAH-dah)—a tortilla filled with meat, cheese, or chicken, rolled and served with a tomato sauce

fajitas (fah-HEE-tahs)—grilled strips of marinated beef or chicken wrapped in a tortilla

Fiesta San Antonio (fee-YES-tah)—"festival"; a holiday celebrated every April in San Antonio

flan (FLAHN)—a caramel custard

frijoles (free-HOH-lais)—beans

Las Posadas (LOHS poh-SAH-dahs)—a Christmas procession

La Villita (LAH vee-YEE-tah)—"the little village"; a reproduction of an 18th-century village in San Antonio

luminarias (loo-mee-NAHR-ee-YAHS)—lanterns made from a paper bag with a lighted candle inside

mariachi (mahr-ee-YAH-chee)—traditional Mexican musician

Paseo del Río (pah-SAY-oh DEL REE-oh)—River Walk

piñata (peen-YAH-tah)—a papier-màché figure filled with candy

tamale (tah-MAH-lay)—cornmeal dough filled with meat, wrapped in cornhusks, and steamed

tortilla (tohr-TEE-yah)—a flat piece of dough, usually made from corn or flour

Index

About the Author

Sally Lee grew to love San Antonio during the 13 years she lived there. The former special education teacher has published several nonfiction books for children and teenagers. She now lives in Sugar Land, Texas, with her husband and two children.